A NOTE TO PARENTS

When your children are ready to "step into reading," giving them the right books—and lots of them—is as crucial as giving them the right food to eat. **Step into Reading Books** present exciting stories and information reinforced with lively, colorful illustrations that make learning to read fun, satisfying, and worthwhile. They are priced so that acquiring an entire library of them is affordable. And they are beginning readers with an important difference—they're written on four levels.

Step 1 Books, with their very large type and extremely simple vocabulary, have been created for the very youngest readers. **Step 2 Books** are both longer and slightly more difficult. **Step 3 Books,** written to mid-second-grade reading levels, are for the child who has acquired even greater reading skills. **Step 4 Books** offer exciting nonfiction for the increasingly proficient reader.

Children develop at different ages. **Step into Reading Books,** with their four levels of reading, are designed to help children become good—and interested—readers *faster.* The grade levels assigned to the four steps—preschool through grade 1 for Step 1, grades 1 through 3 for Step 2, grades 2 and 3 for Step 3, and grades 2 through 4 for Step 4—are intended only as guides. Some children move through all four steps very rapidly; others climb the steps over a period of several years. These books will help your child "step into reading" in style!

Text copyright © 1988 by Random House, Inc. Illustrations copyright © 1988 by Lynn
Munsinger. All rights reserved under International and Pan-American Copyright Conventions.
Published in the United States by Random House, Inc., New York, and simultaneously in
Canada by Random House of Canada Limited, Toronto.

Library of Congress Cataloging-in-Publication Data: Hayward, Linda. Hello, house! (Step into
reading. A Step 1 book) Adaptation of: Heyo house / Joel Chandler Harris. SUMMARY: A simple
retelling of one of the "Tales of Uncle Remus" in which Brer Wolf hides in Brer Rabbit's
house in order to capture him when he comes home. [1. Folklore, Afro-American. 2. Animals—
Folklore] I. Munsinger, Lynn, ill. II. Title. III. Series: Step into reading. Step 1 book.
PZ8.1.H3245He 1988 398.2 [E] 86-22080 ISBN: 0-394-88864-2 (pbk.); 0-394-98864-7 (lib. bdg.)

Manufactured in the United States of America   13   14   15   16   17   18   19   20

STEP INTO READING is a trademark of Random House, Inc.

Step into Reading

HELLO, HOUSE!

By Linda Hayward
Illustrated by Lynn Munsinger

A Step 1 Book

Random House New York

Brer Wolf is
full of ways
to get
Brer Rabbit.

Brer Rabbit is
full of ways
to trick
Brer Wolf.

Brer Wolf
is bigger.

But
Brer Rabbit
is a whole
lot smarter.

One day Brer Rabbit
and Mrs. Rabbit
and the little Rabs
go on a picnic.

Brer Wolf hides
in their house.
He will catch
Brer Rabbit this time.

By and by
Brer Rabbit
comes back.

He feels funny.
Why is the door open?

Brer Rabbit peeks
in the window.
But he doesn't
see anything.

Brer Rabbit listens
at the chimney.
But he doesn't
hear anything.

Brer Rabbit steps up
to the door.
Does he go inside?
No!
Brer Rabbit has
more sense
than that!

Instead
he begins
to holler.
"HELLO, HOUSE!"

Brer Wolf is surprised.

Can houses talk?

Brer Wolf waits.

Brer Wolf listens.

But the house doesn't
say anything.

"Something is wrong!"
shouts Brer Rabbit.

"The house doesn't say
'HELLO TO YOU TOO!'"

"HELLO TO YOU TOO!"
calls Brer Wolf
in a low voice.

Brer Rabbit chuckles.

Now he knows something.

He knows Brer Wolf

is in his house!

"That house
talks too low,"
shouts Brer Rabbit.

"HELLO TO YOU TOO!"
calls Brer Wolf
in a high voice.

"That house
talks too high,"
shouts Brer Rabbit.

"HELLO TO YOU TOO!"
calls Brer Wolf
in a voice
not too high
and not too low.

"Brer Wolf!"
says Brer Rabbit.
"You can try and try.
But you will never
sound like a house."

Brer Wolf is mad!

Now he knows something.

He knows Brer Rabbit

has tricked him again!

Brer Wolf comes out.

He runs off.

He is glad

to get away

from Brer Rabbit

and his tricks.

Brer Rabbit
and his family
go inside.
"Hello, house!"
says Brer Rabbit.
But the house
doesn't say anything.

Houses don't talk,
you know!